*First published
in Great Britain by
HarperCollins
Children's Books
in 2008*

1 3 5 7 9 10 8 6 4 2
*ISBN 10: 0-00-725312-5
ISBN 13: 978-0-00-725312-8*

*Visit Roary at www.roarytheracingcar.com*

*Printed and bound in Italy
By Rotolito Lombarda SpA*

HarperCollins *Children's Books*

# Roary the Racing Car
# Annual 2009

# CONTENTS

>> Page 10 – Starting Grid

>> Page 12 – Roary's First Day Read Along Story

>> Page 34 – Meet the Gang!

>> Page 36 – Motor Car A-Z

>> Page 37 – Silver Hatch Crossword

>> Page 38 – Indoor Fun!

>> Page 39 – Colouring In

>> Page 40 – Matching Pairs Game

>> Page 42 – Special Delivery Read Along Story

>> Page 50 – Colouring In

>> Page 52 – Silver Hatch Race Game

>> Page 54 – More Indoor Fun!

>> Page 56 – Wordsearch

>> Page 57 – Design a Silver Hatch Star!

>> Page 59 – Colouring In

>> Page 60 – Marsha's Maze

>> Page 61 – Answers

Hello there, I'm Roary the Racing Car!

Would you like to hear what happened on my first day at Silver Hatch racetrack? There's a funny story about it inside!

There are also lots of games and fun things to do in this Roary the Racing Car Annual. And there are some great pictures for you to colour in yourself, too.

There's even a recipe for Flash's favourite carrot cake! First, though, why don't you read along with me about my first day at the racetrack?

# Roary's First Day

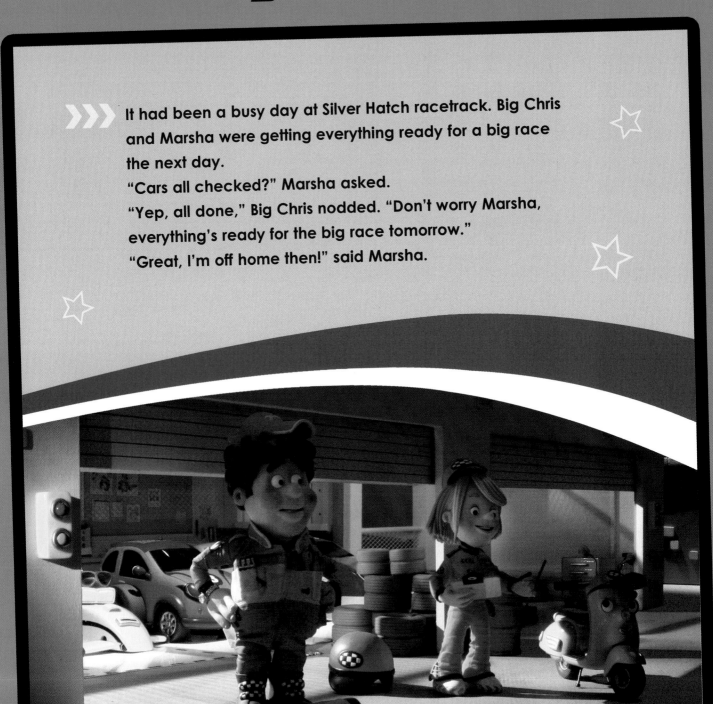

It had been a busy day at Silver Hatch racetrack. Big Chris and Marsha were getting everything ready for a big race the next day.

"Cars all checked?" Marsha asked.

"Yep, all done," Big Chris nodded. "Don't worry Marsha, everything's ready for the big race tomorrow."

"Great, I'm off home then!" said Marsha.

"Phew, what a day," said Big Chris. Just as he was about to lock up the garage, he heard a strange revving noise inside.

>>>

In the workshop, all the cars were happily fast asleep.
All the cars except for one.
Over in the furthest bay, Big Chris spotted Roary, revving and shaking in his sleep.
"**Ahh!**" yelled Roary, waking with a start. "Big Chris! I crashed in the middle of the big race!"
"It's okay, Roary," Big Chris gently patted his bonnet to try and calm him down. "You just had a bad dream."

"I can't race tomorrow, Big Chris," Roary said nervously.
"I'm scared I'll mess it up, just like in my dream!"
"No you won't, Roary," smiled Big Chris. "How's about I tell you
a story to help you get back to sleep?"
"Yes, please," giggled Roary, settling back down.
"Okay, so it was Roary's very first day in Silver Hatch..."
Big Chris began.

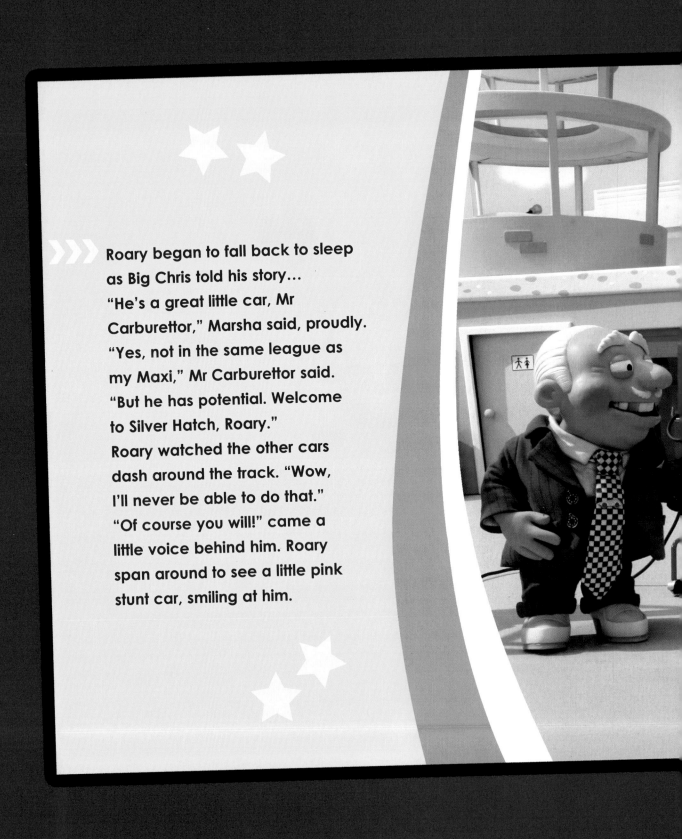

Roary began to fall back to sleep as Big Chris told his story...

"He's a great little car, Mr Carburettor," Marsha said, proudly. "Yes, not in the same league as my Maxi," Mr Carburettor said. "But he has potential. Welcome to Silver Hatch, Roary."

Roary watched the other cars dash around the track. "Wow, I'll never be able to do that."

"Of course you will!" came a little voice behind him. Roary span around to see a little pink stunt car, smiling at him.

"I'm Cici," she said. "And you must be Roary."

"Y-y-yes," Roary stuttered. She was very pretty. "Er, do you race too?"

"Yes and so will you," she said. "I'm off to do some practice laps but I'll be back to see how you are later. Au revoir!"

She zoomed off around the track, leaving Roary to stare after her.

>>> Soon, Big Chris was hard at work on Roary, prepping him for the race. "Welcome to your new home, Roary," he said. "This is where my number one star will sleep!"

Roary smiled. "Your number one star? Oh, thanks, Big Chris!"

Big Chris gave him a big grin in return and started playing with his engine.

"Ooh, that **tickles!**" laughed Roary.

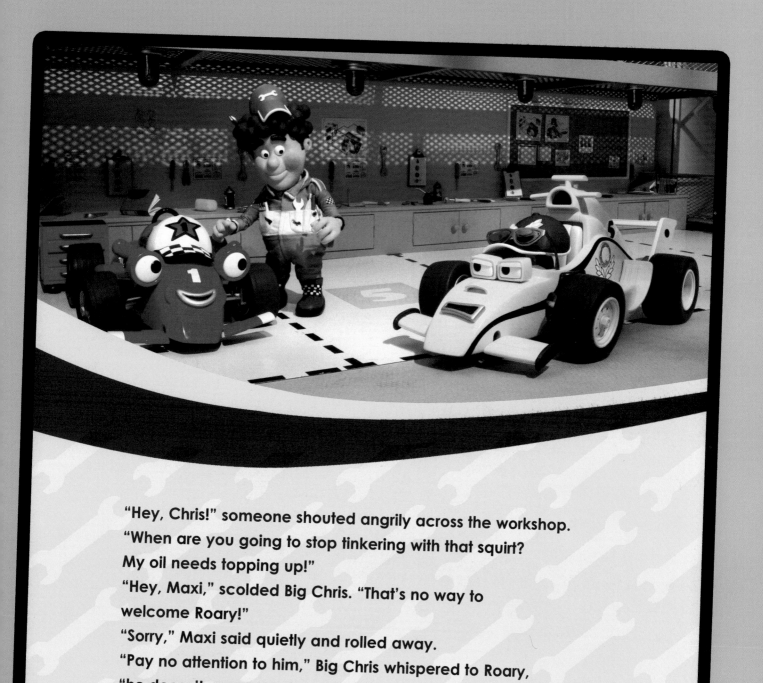

"Hey, Chris!" someone shouted angrily across the workshop. "When are you going to stop tinkering with that squirt? My oil needs topping up!"

"Hey, Maxi," scolded Big Chris. "That's no way to welcome Roary!"

"Sorry," Maxi said quietly and rolled away.

"Pay no attention to him," Big Chris whispered to Roary, "he doesn't mean any harm."

>>> In no time at all, Roary was ready to test out his engine.
"Hello, Roary," called Cici. "How's it going, Big Chris?"
"I'm all done with Roary," Big Chris said, "why don't you show him around?"
"Love to!" grinned Cici. "How are you settling in?"
"I don't think I belong here," Roary said sadly as they rolled out on to the track. "I'm not a proper racing car."
"You look like one to me!" Cici said. "Come on, I'll show you around Silver Hatch."

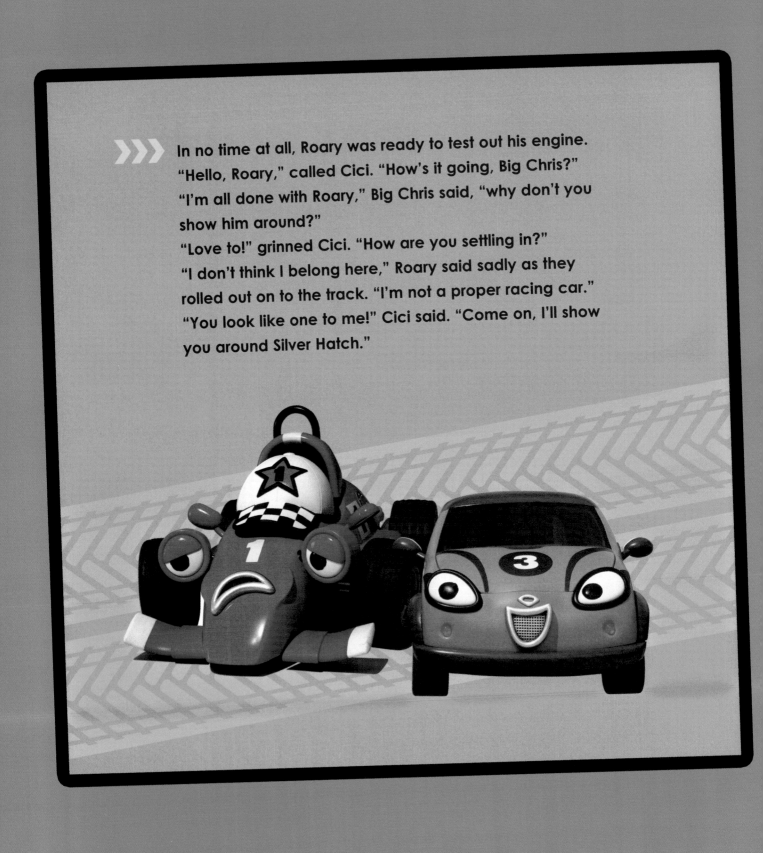

"This is Rusty," she said, pointing towards a large, old-looking caravan, "where Big Chris lives."
"Keep the noise down!" Rusty muttered, opening one eye.
"Oh, you must be the new arrival, sorry, just getting my beauty sleep."
Roary looked over at Cici and giggled.

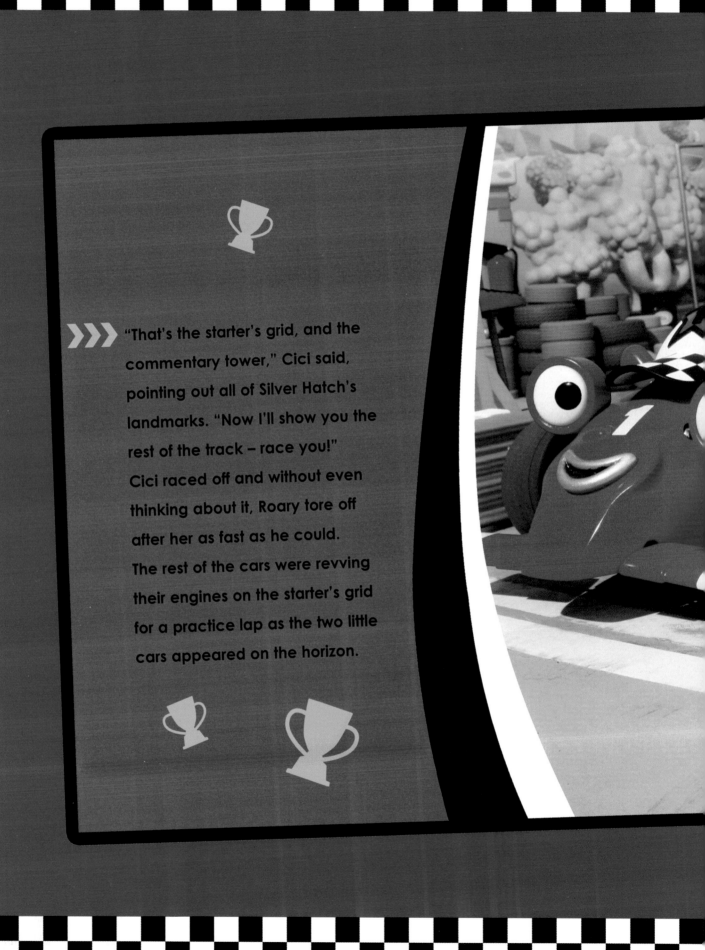

"That's the starter's grid, and the commentary tower," Cici said, pointing out all of Silver Hatch's landmarks. "Now I'll show you the rest of the track – race you!" Cici raced off and without even thinking about it, Roary tore off after her as fast as he could. The rest of the cars were revving their engines on the starter's grid for a practice lap as the two little cars appeared on the horizon.

"Okay," Big Chris said to Maxi, Drifter and Tin Top as they lined up. "I want you to do one last practice lap to check your engines are running smoothly."

As the flag went down, they set off with roaring engines and whizzing tyres, quickly followed by Roary and Cici!

"That's my boy," smiled Big Chris.

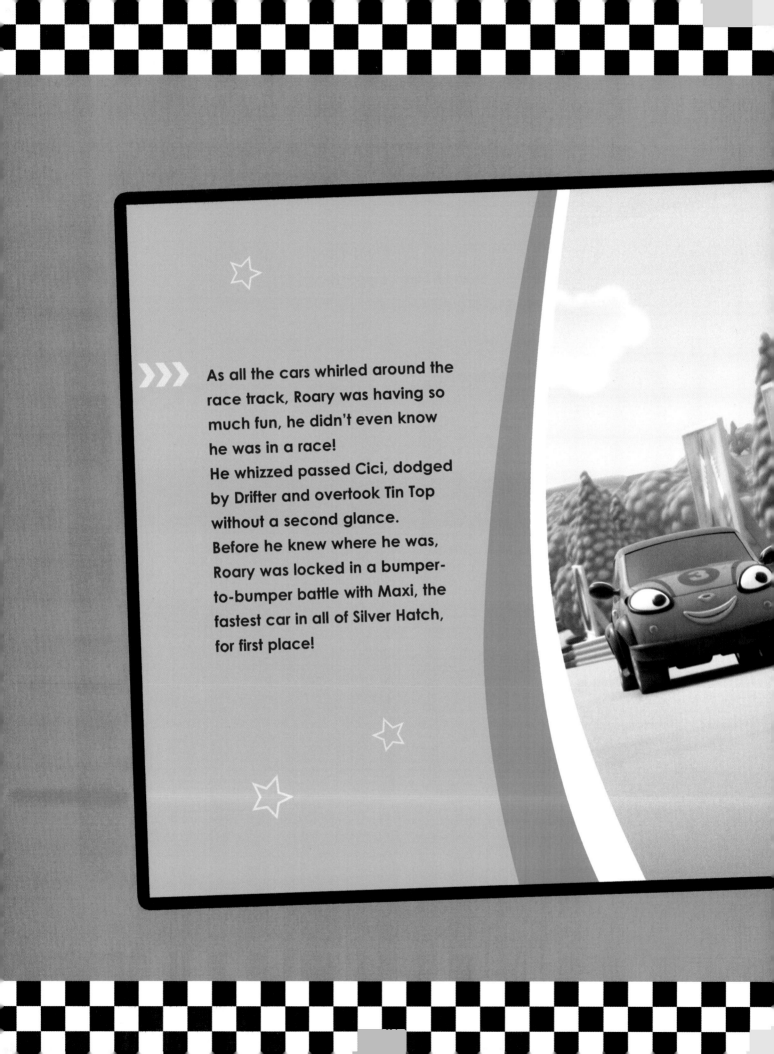

As all the cars whirled around the race track, Roary was having so much fun, he didn't even know he was in a race!
He whizzed passed Cici, dodged by Drifter and overtook Tin Top without a second glance.
Before he knew where he was, Roary was locked in a bumper-to-bumper battle with Maxi, the fastest car in all of Silver Hatch, for first place!

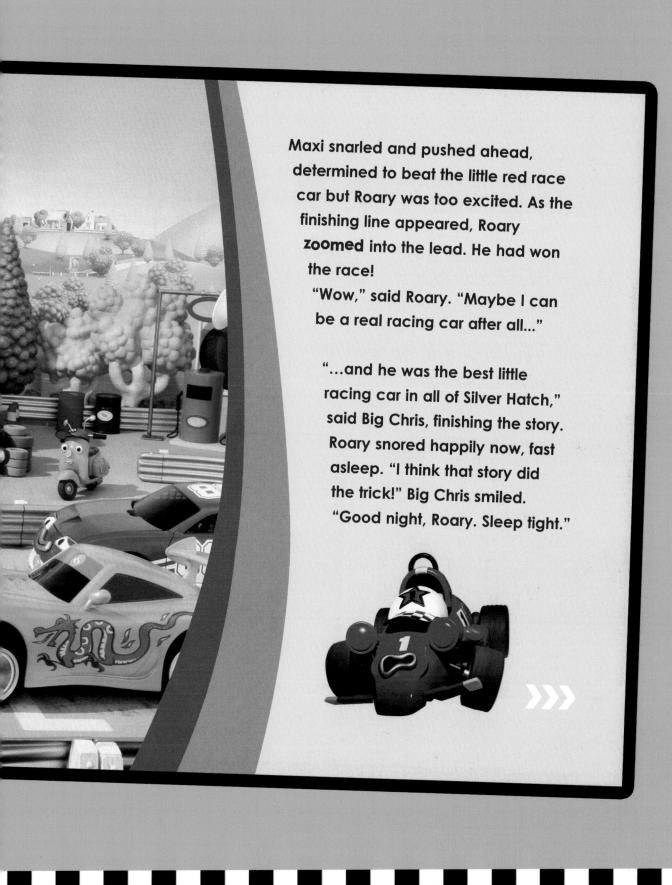

Maxi snarled and pushed ahead, determined to beat the little red race car but Roary was too excited. As the finishing line appeared, Roary **zoomed** into the lead. He had won the race!

"Wow," said Roary. "Maybe I can be a real racing car after all..."

"...and he was the best little racing car in all of Silver Hatch," said Big Chris, finishing the story. Roary snored happily now, fast asleep. "I think that story did the trick!" Big Chris smiled.

"Good night, Roary. Sleep tight."

The next morning, Roary woke bright and early, all excited about the big race. "Morning everyone!" he called out to the other cars. "Ready for the big race?"

"Mamma mia," groaned Maxi, "I have to be perfect. My oil, my oil…"

"My tyres feel flat," said Drifter. "I won't be able to glide around corners!"

"What if I don't beat my lap time?" fretted Cici.

"I just know I'm gonna crash!" moaned Tin Top.

"Don't worry everyone!" said Roary cheerfully. "It's okay to be nervous. Maybe I can tell you a story about a brave little red racing car?"

And so Roary told the others how he overcame his nerves on his first day at Silver Hatch. The other cars forgot all their worries and even began to look forward to the big race!

# Meet the Gang!

These are my friends, Maxi, Cici, Tin Top and Drifter. They're the best racing cars in all the world!

35

# Motor car A-Z

You can play this game anywhere, and it's especially good for when you're on a long journey somewhere!

Pick one of the characters from Silver Hatch and write down the letters of their name on a piece of paper, one above the other, in a column. Now look out for something that begins with the same letters, in the correct order. If you play with ROARY, you first have to spot something that begins with R, and then something else that begins with O, and so on.

Only the first person to spot an object ticks off their letter, or writes the word next to it on the list. The first one to complete their name wins!

# Silver Hatch Crossword

**Across**
3. What is Marsha's job?
6. Special cup for the winner!
7. Where we go if we need help during a race

**Down**
1. What do we use to stop?
2. What does Marsha wave when we race?
3. What is Big Chris's job?
4. What is Silver Hatch beach covered in?
5. We start the race at the starting ----
8. The things we wear on our wheels

# Indoor Fun

Quick as a Flash Carrot Cake:
Serves: 6
Ingredients:
- 2 cups sugar
- 2 cups flour
- 2 teaspoons baking soda
- 1 cup oil
- 4 eggs
- 3 cups grated carrots
- 2 teaspoons cinnamon
- 1 teaspoon salt
- 1/2 cup nuts

Preparation:
1. Add the oil to the dry ingredients and mix well.
2. Then add the eggs, one at a time, stirring all the time.
3. Finally, stir in the carrots and the nuts.
4. Pour into a cake tin and bake at 350 degrees F for 35 minutes – don't forget to get a grown up to help with the oven!

Colour this picture of me and my friend, Flash!

# Matching Pairs Game

Can you see
which two pictures
of Big Chris
match exactly?

# Special Delivery

It was a beautiful day, and Roary was on his way to Farmer Green's farm. Big Chris had run out of milk for his tea.

"Morning, Farmer Green," said Roary, as he drove in.

"Morning, Roary," replied Farmer Green. "What can I do for you?"

"I'd like some milk for Big Chris, please," said Roary.

"No problem! I'll just get you some," said Farmer Green, going into the shop and coming out with a bottle, "No race today?"

"No," said Roary, "it's going to be a nice quiet day today."

Farmer Green looked envious. "Not for me; I've got lots of deliveries to make!" he said. But when he tried to start FB, there was no engine sound. Just a sort of clunk.

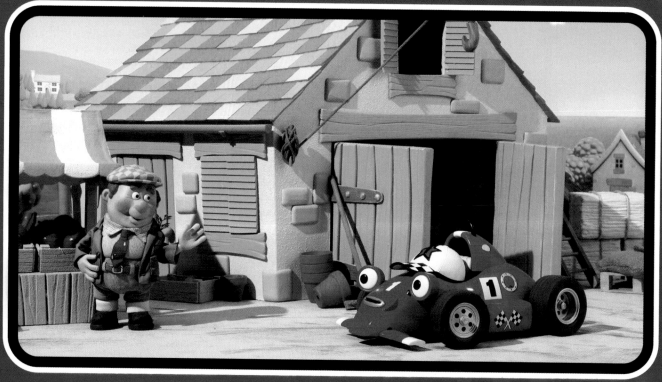

"I think there's something wrong with FB, Farmer Green," said Roary.
"Shall I ask Big Chris to come and get him with Plugger?"
"That's good of you, Roary," replied Farmer Green, "He's obviously
not going anywhere otherwise. But how will I make my deliveries?"
"I'll help," said Roary.
"Thanks, Roary, you are kind. But the thing is, you're rather small.
And I've got an awful lot to deliver!"
"Well, I'll ask if the other cars will help, too," said Roary, helpfully,
and zoomed off.

He was soon back at the track. He told Big Chris about FB and Farmer Green, and Big Chris had an idea.

"How about Plugger? He's got a lot of space in the back, and we're not racing today, so once he's brought FB here he could go back and help Farmer Green!"

So Big Chris and Plugger went over to the farm. While he was hitching up FB, Big Chris explained his idea, and Farmer Green cheered up immediately.

"Thanks, Big Chris! Plugger will be perfect!" he said.

Off they went to the workshop. Big Chris unhitched FB, and soon Plugger was back at the farm being loaded up with groceries.

"It'll make a nice change to see some happy customers, instead of just broken cars," he laughed as they set off.

Meanwhile, Big Chris was checking FB.

"Oh dear," he said. "I think it's been a while since FB was serviced. His engine's going to have to be replaced with a new one. Trouble is, I haven't got the right sort here. We'll have to get one in. Unfortunately, only Plugger is big enough to carry it..."

"And he's making Farmer Green's deliveries." Roary finished Big Chris's sentence. "Oh dear." He thought for a minute, then continued, "Well, I'll go and get him back. Do you need any of the other cars today? Only if we all helped, maybe we could do the deliveries."

"I'm going to be too busy with FB to do anything else," said Big Chris, "What do you all think?"

"No problem," they all cried! Except Maxi, who grumbled, "Well, if I'm not going to get any attention here..." They all laughed, and one by one they rolled out of the workshop and down the track towards the farm.

But Plugger wasn't at the farm. He was already out making deliveries.

"I didn't think of that," said Roary. "Now what will we do? He could be anywhere in the village!"

Drifter thought. "We'll split up and look around the village. Then, whoever finds Plugger will tell him to toot his horn. The rest of us will follow the sound, and then we can take over the deliveries."

"Brilliant," chorused the other cars, and set off down the road.

They drove around the village, looking for Farmer Green and Plugger. Eventually Roary found them. He told Farmer Green about the engine.

"But how am I going to get the rest of my deliveries done without Plugger?" asked Farmer Green.

"Don't worry," said Roary, "The other cars are here in the village too. If Plugger toots his horn, they'll hear him and follow the sound. Then we can all help you!" So Plugger tooted his horn, and soon all the cars were there. Farmer Green unloaded Plugger and he dashed off to pick up the new engine. One at a time, the cars took the groceries to Farmer Green's customers. In the meantime, Plugger found the engine he needed and took it back to the farm.

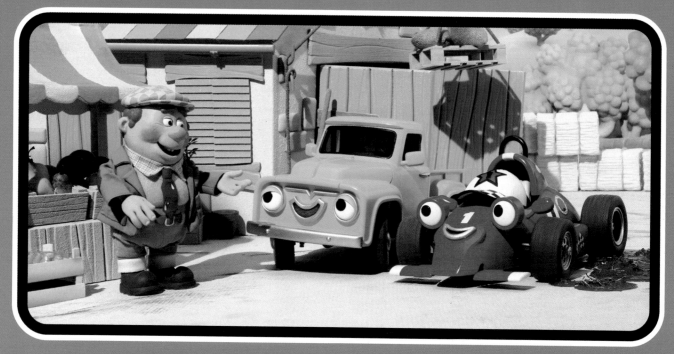

"Thanks, Plugger," said Big Chris, "Now, while I fit this, you can go and help the others finish the deliveries." But by the time Plugger arrived, they were all done. Farmer Green was beaming!

"Thank you," he said, "I don't know what I would have done without you!" The cars were pleased with themselves as well; it had been a busy day for a day off but they had all enjoyed themselves – even Maxi!

Plugger took Farmer Green to the workshop, with all the other cars following. Big Chris had fitted FB's new engine and he was raring to go. "You've all been so helpful today," said Farmer Green, "thank you. What a wonderful team you make! Tomorrow, FB and I will bring you all a very special delivery to show how grateful we are. Won't we, FB?" "Definitely," grinned FB. "But now, let's test my new engine!" Farmer Green got into FB's cab and they whizzed back to the farm. "Well done, everyone," said Big Chris, "What a good day! Perhaps I can have that cup of tea now!" All the cars laughed. It had been a good day. And Big Chris definitely deserved his cup of tea!

Here's a busy scene at the racetrack.
Colour it in using all your favourite colours!

# Silver Hatch Race Game

START

Using a die and different coloured counters throw a six to start. Race your friends around the track, taking turns to throw and following the instructions on the squares you land on.

Too fast! You skidded off the track. Miss a go while you wait for Plugger.

Dinkie on the track – go back one place.

# Indoor Fun

Here are two pictures of me and my friends. There are five differences between the two pictures. See if you can spot what they are and colour them in (the answers are upside down at the bottom of the page!) Then colour in the rest of the pictures!

# Wordsearch

See if you can find the names of me
and some of my friends in the box below.
Names can read forwards, backwards, up,
down and diagonally.

| | | | | | | | | | | | | | |
|---|---|---|---|---|---|---|---|---|---|---|---|---|---|
| N | A | M | S | O | N | O | R | B | D | Y | H | Z | X | Z |
| G | V | K | I | M | O | C | E | L | O | M | N | O | P | J |
| E | L | Q | R | R | T | P | U | U | G | H | S | A | L | F |
| X | S | V | H | Y | E | I | O | P | X | T | L | J | R | Q |
| I | G | O | C | N | M | G | N | H | G | S | W | V | Z | X |
| R | N | Q | G | S | Z | O | G | T | Y | Y | B | K | J | A |
| D | B | Y | I | L | D | A | K | U | O | J | M | Y | Y | Z |
| V | R | S | B | L | T | H | B | Q | L | P | U | R | M | Z |
| V | O | I | D | I | N | K | I | E | G | P | A | I | U | X |
| V | A | W | F | I | C | I | C | L | V | O | I | M | G | R |
| M | A | X | I | T | K | D | I | D | R | K | I | A | P | B |
| T | I | U | A | F | E | B | G | Z | L | B | I | R | R | A |
| Y | I | W | X | Y | Q | R | L | H | W | W | C | S | M | E |
| R | V | A | K | K | K | H | Y | G | B | B | P | H | N | P |
| O | C | I | O | Q | F | I | W | E | N | U | L | A | W | I |

BIG CHRIS
CICI
DINKIE
DRIFTER
FLASH
MARSHA
MAXI
MOLECOM
PLUGGER
ROARY
TINTOP

# Design a Silver Hatch Star

**Can you design a new car to race with me at Silver Hatch?**

Do you remember the first story in this book, about my very first day at the track? Here's a picture of me and Big Chris from it to colour in, using your favourite pencils, pens or crayons.

# Marsha's maze

Marsha has lost her marshall's flag again.
Can you help her to find them by following this maze?